THE AMERICAN JOURNEY
THE SYRIAN-AMERICAN
JOURNEY

by Rachel Castro

Ideas for Parents and Teachers

Pogo Books let children practice reading informational text while introducing them to nonfiction features such as headings, labels, sidebars, maps, and diagrams, as well as a table of contents, glossary, and index.

Carefully leveled text with a strong photo match offers early fluent readers the support they need to succeed.

Before Reading

- "Walk" through the book and point out the various nonfiction features. Ask the student what purpose each feature serves.
- Look at the glossary together. Read and discuss the words.

Read the Book

- Have the child read the book independently.
- Invite him or her to list questions that arise from reading.

After Reading

- Discuss the child's questions. Talk about how he or she might find answers to those questions.
- Prompt the child to think more. Ask: Do you know any Syrian Americans? How are their cultural traditions similar to or different from yours?

Pogo Books are published by Jump!
5357 Penn Avenue South
Minneapolis, MN 55419
www.jumplibrary.com

Library of Congress Cataloging-in-Publication Data

Names: Castro, Rachel, author.
Title: The Syrian-American journey / Rachel Castro
Description: Minneapolis, MN: Pogo Books, published by Jump!, 2020. | Series: The American journey
Includes bibliographical references and index.
Identifiers: LCCN 2019000177 (print)
LCCN 2019004688 (ebook)
ISBN 9781641289245 (ebook)
ISBN 9781641289184 (hardcover : alk. paper)
ISBN 9781641289207 (pbk.)
Subjects: LCSH: Syrian Americans—Juvenile literature.
Syria—History—Civil War, 2011—Refugees—Juvenile literature.
Syria—Emigration and immigration—Juvenile literature.
United States—Emigration and immigration—Juvenile literature.
Classification: LCC E184.S98 (ebook)
LCC E184.S98 C38 2020 (print) | DDC 956.9104/23—dc23
LC record available at https://lccn.loc.gov/2019000177

Editor: Susanne Bushman
Designer: Molly Ballanger
Content Consultant: Dr. Silva Mathema,
Senior Policy Analyst, Center for American Progress

Photo Credits: Smallcreative/Shutterstock, cover (tl); Dancestrokes/Shutterstock, cover (tr); Pixfiction/Shutterstock, cover (bl), cover (br); Michael Honegger/Alamy, 1; Amir Sabbagh/Shutterstock, 3; Jose_Matheus/Shutterstock, 4; Konevi/Shutterstock, 5; Nicolas Economou/Shutterstock, 6-7; Anadolu Agency/Getty, 8-9; dinosmichail/iStock, 10; Orlok/Shutterstock, 11; Karin Laub/AP Images, 12-13; FREDERIC J. BROWN/Getty, 14-15; sumroeng chinnapan/Shutterstock, 16; Zurijeta/iStock, 17; tbralnina/iStock, 18-19; FatCamera/iStock, 20-21; MicroStockHub/iStock, 23.

Printed in the United States of America at Corporate Graphics in North Mankato, Minnesota.

TABLE OF CONTENTS

CHAPTER 1

LIFE IN SYRIA

Syria is in the Middle East. Most people here speak Arabic. The **capital** is Damascus. It is one of the oldest cities in the world!

Damascus

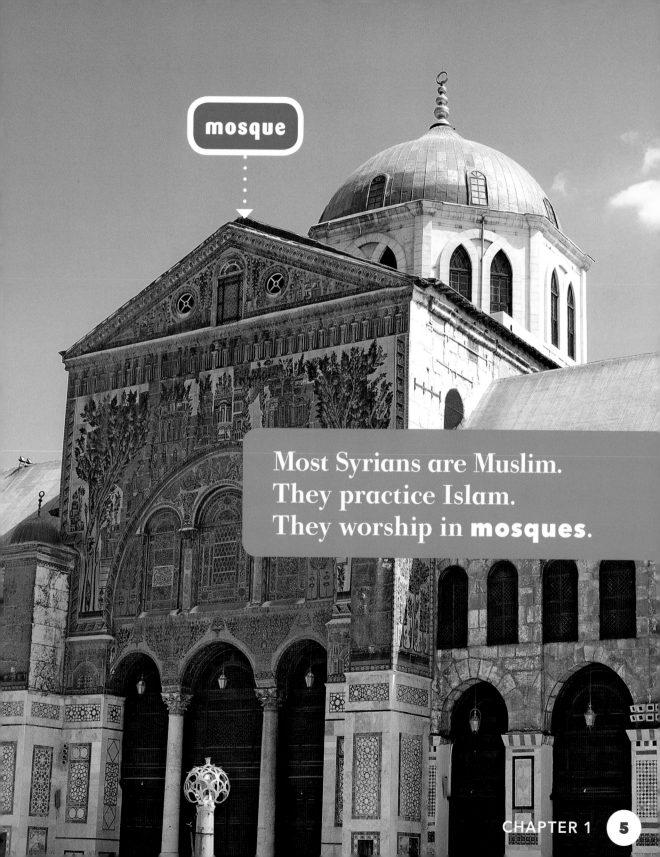

mosque

Most Syrians are Muslim.
They practice Islam.
They worship in **mosques**.

The Syrian government was unfair. Syrians **protested**. A **civil war** began in 2011. Since then, many Syrians have fled. Some were ordered to leave. Many left on boats. Some walked. They became **refugees**.

Most fled to nearby countries. Some went to Lebanon or Jordan. About 3.6 million went to Turkey.

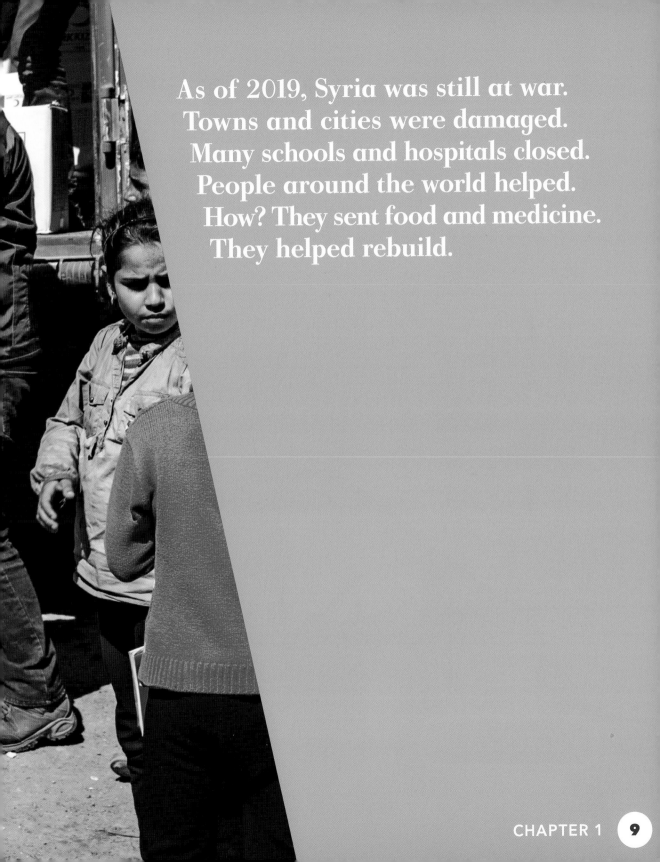

As of 2019, Syria was still at war.
Towns and cities were damaged.
Many schools and hospitals closed.
People around the world helped.
How? They sent food and medicine.
They helped rebuild.

CHAPTER 2

COMING TO AMERICA

As of 2018, about 13 million Syrians lived in temporary homes. About 10 percent are in **refugee camps**. These are crowded. Clean water is limited. Many people get sick.

refugee camp

Refugees may go back to Syria.
Or they stay where they are.
They may move to a new country.

Syrian refugees who come to the United States go through **background checks**. This can take two years. There are many interviews. Syrians must pass many checks. Others have come here for **asylum**.

LEARN THE CULTURE!

Syrians take off their shoes when they enter mosques. Then they wash their feet. Why? This is a prayer **ritual**.

background check

Some U.S. states have more Syrians than others. These are California, Michigan, and Texas. Why? Many have family in these states. These are also good places to find jobs.

TAKE A LOOK!

Take a look at how many Syrian refugees came here from 2014 to 2018! Which year had the most? Which year had the least?

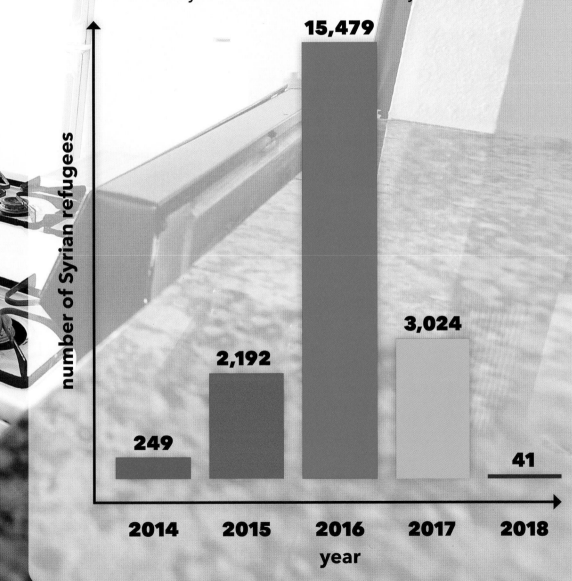

number of Syrian refugees

15,479

3,024

2,192

249

41

2014   2015   2016   2017   2018

year

CHAPTER 3

A NEW HOME

The U.S. government helps refugees. How? It gives them **loans**. This money helps them travel here.

Kids start new schools. They study English. It can be hard. They can face **prejudice**. Some are treated unfairly.

hummus

Syrian refugees keep parts of their **culture**. One is called mezze. This is a special way of dining. Food is shared. Dishes can include hummus and yogurt.

WHAT DO YOU THINK?

Cultures are different. Refugees can feel pressure to fit in. How can we respect their cultures?

They can apply for **green cards** after one year. They can become U.S. **citizens** after five years. Then they can vote! They can also help family members come here.

Syrian Americans are our friends. They are our neighbors. We all call this country home.

DID YOU KNOW?

Syrian refugees succeed around the world! Amineh Abou Kerech won a prize for poetry. She was 13 years old! Yusra Mardini swam in the Olympics! She was on the Refugee Olympic Team.

QUICK FACTS & TOOLS

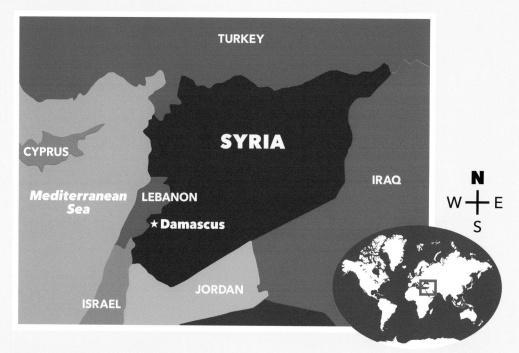

Number of Syrians displaced around the world as of 2018: about 13 million

Number of displaced Syrians in Europe as of 2017: about 1 million

Number of Syrians displaced within Syria as of 2018: 6.2 million

Most common countries for relocation: Turkey, Lebanon, Jordan, Iraq, Egypt

Number of Syrian refugees in the United States as of 2018: about 21,000

Most common U.S. states for relocation: California, Michigan, Texas

asylum: A form of protection for refugees who fear harm in their home country because of their race, religion, political beliefs, or other affiliations.

background checks: Processes of collecting information to see what people have done in the past.

capital: A city where government leaders meet.

citizens: People who have full rights in a certain country, such as the right to work and the right to vote.

civil war: A war between people living in the same country.

culture: The ideas, customs, traditions, and ways of life of a group of people.

displaced: Out of one's home because of war, violence, or famine.

green cards: Permits, called Lawful Permanent Resident Cards, that allow immigrants and refugees to live in the United States permanently.

loans: Borrowed money that must be paid back.

mosques: Buildings used for worship by Muslims.

prejudice: An opinion that is formed about a person or a group of people before getting to know them.

protested: Demonstrated against something.

refugee camps: Temporary settlements that house people who had to leave their homes.

refugees: People who leave their home countries because of war, violence, or disaster.

ritual: An act or series of acts that is always performed the same way.

INDEX

TO LEARN MORE

Finding more information is as easy as 1, 2, 3.

❶ Go to www.factsurfer.com

❷ Enter "Syrian-Americanjourney" into the search box.

❸ Choose your cover to see a list of websites.

FACT SURFER